For Juliette and Merlin, my two rainbows
D.S.

Plip, the Umbrella Man
by David Sire and Thomas Baas

Translation from French by David Wilson

Published by Little Gestalten, Berlin 2014
ISBN: 978-3-89955-738-1
Typeface: Century by Tony Stan
Printed by Eberl Print, Immenstadt \ Made in Germany

The French original edition L'homme Parapluie *was published by Éditions Sarbacane.*
© for the French edition: Éditions Sarbacane, Paris 2013
© for the English edition: Little Gestalten, an imprint of Die Gestalten Verlag Gmbh & Co. KG, Berlin 2014
English translation rights arranged through La Petite Agence, Paris.

For more information, please visit little.gestalten.com.

Bibliographic information published by the Deutsche Nationalbibliothek.
The Deutsche Nationalbibliothek lists this publication in the Deutsche Nationalbibliografie;
detailed bibliographic data are available online at http://dnb.d-nb.de.

This book was printed on paper certified according to the standard of FSC®.

Gestalten is a climate-neutral company. We collaborate with the non-profit carbon offset provider
myclimate (www.myclimate.org) to neutralize the company's carbon footprint produced through
our worldwide business activities by investing in projects that reduce CO_2 emissions
(www.gestalten.com/myclimate).

David Sire
Thomas Baas

LITTLE
GESTALTEN

When he was born,
Plip had a normal human head.

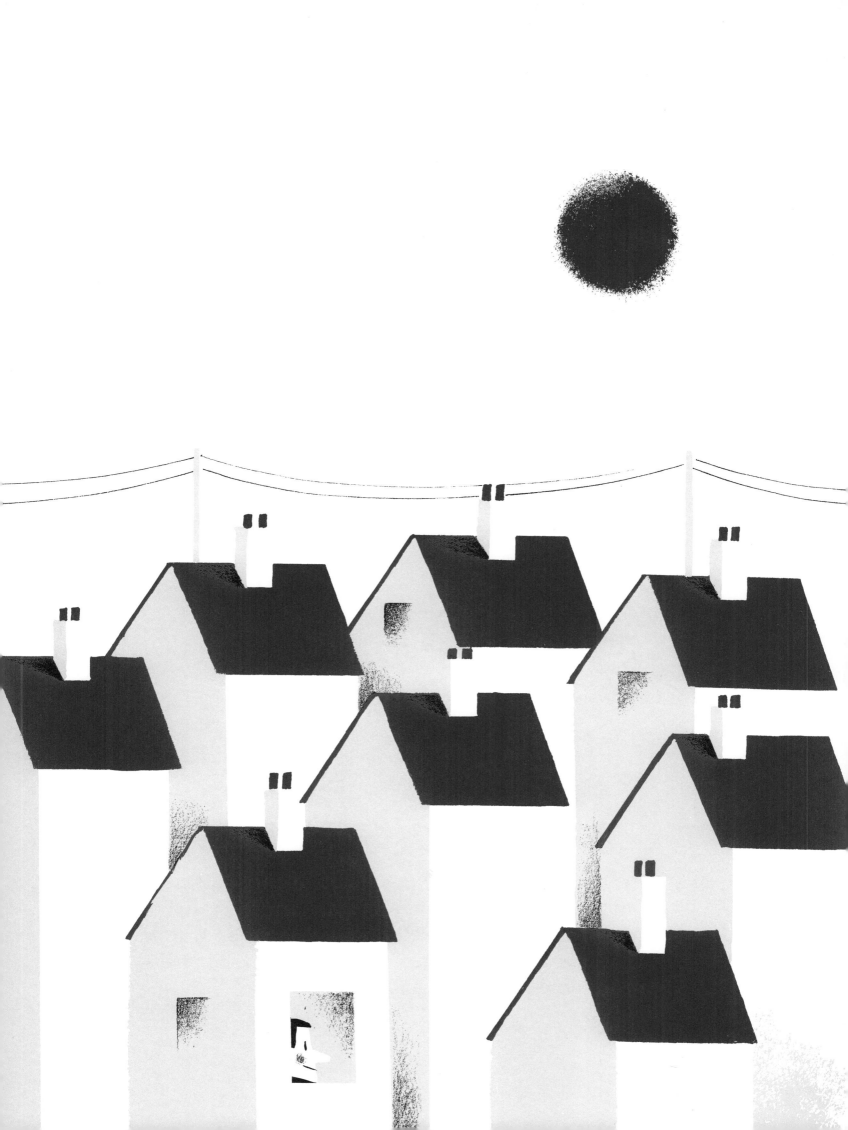

But then the rain came.

At first Plip didn't take much notice, thinking the rain would stop. But the rain was stubborn. It chased him wherever he went, and it always caught up with him. Day after day, night after night, the rain fell in heavy drops down onto his head.

Soon Plip found himself soaked to the skin,
and his mouth was the wrong way up.
When he realized that very soon his heart
would catch cold, Plip decided to become
an umbrella man.

For a while he lived a waterproof life as
an umbrella man. He could hear the rain falling.
He could hear his heart drying out.

Sometimes, it's true, he felt a bit lonely.
"Never mind," he said to himself, "you can't have everything, and under here at least I'm dry."

And so Plip carried on living in silence under his large umbrella.

One morning, he came face to face with an umbrella woman. "Good heavens above!" she cried. "Look how alike we are! How about the two of us getting together, eh?"

Plip had a funny feeling, but he said yes without giving it much thought.

Only how on earth could they do it?
Umbrellas getting together are more embarrassing than embracing.

The umbrella woman was already imagining swarms of baby umbrellas. She had fallen in love with Plip, and was laughing like a babbling brook.

But Plip wasn't laughing.

With a dry clunk he closed himself up and ran far,
far into the distance, shouting, "Go away!"

Deep within him raged a tempest which swept aside everything that was in his way. Tempest, tornado, typhoon ... Plip was carried off, umbrella head over umbrella heels!

And it rained as never before – a veritable flood.
The waters rose faster and faster, and Plip staggered
along, exhausted. He didn't know what to do with
this bathtub head in which fish-questions were
swimming to and fro.

He closed his eyes.

Two small, salty drops. Two small, forgotten drops.
Plip was crying. He had thought he was no longer
able to cry, and yet the tears came back to him of their
own accord. And crying did him good.
All that water inside him – it couldn't go on rising.

And so Plip removed the plug ...

And out poured all his feelings.

In a huge cascade of water and words, his bathtub head
emptied itself to the very last drop.

At his feet the fish-questions quivered, panic-stricken,
then they died, suffocated. Serves them right, thought Plip.
I'm better off without them.

He felt light-headed, a little drunk. Relieved.

Gently he turned his umbrella head.
He transformed it into a kite and sent it soaring
towards the clouds. Those strange clouds that
made the raindrops fall and made men cry.

One by one Plip looked them in the eye and
bade them farewell.

Then he wound the kite back in. At the end of the
string was a surprise present: a very beautiful,
very round balloon ... He unfolded its paper petals,
and then slowly leaned over his reflection in the pool.

Plip trembled to the depths of his being: in the waters of the ancient rain, a large mouth which was the right way up sang its first little drop of liberty.

And Plip went plop.